CONTENTS

JARVIS NIXON

Liberty and Justice Prevails: The Star-Spangled Tangle

CHAPTER ONE

Patriotic Mission

Jarvis Nixon was eleven now. He had come to be kind of famous for fighting crime in his hometown of Auburn, Alabama. Some thought of him as a celebrity, snapping pictures of him anytime they saw him out and about and buzzing about whatever latest brand of tennis shoes he was wearing. Some even went so far as to call him a superhero. Others just liked hanging out with him. Deep inside, he was still the same ole kid he used to be for he had vowed long ago, never to let his crime-fighting abilities go to his head.

There was one thing that was different from when he was a youngster though. He used to go by "Jarvis". Through the years, when his powers kicked in, his name turned to "Justice" because that was exactly what he represented...justice and the American way. It seemed he was always busy fighting crime of one kind or another. So, eventually, to save time and trouble, everyone started calling him "Justice" all the time.

Although Justice had no brothers or sisters on his mother

side, he sort of did. He had a black and white spotted dog named Liberty who was closer to him than his own shadow. Liberty was Justice's partner in fighting crime. "I'm Batman and you're Robin," Justice often told Liberty. Liberty would look at him with big brown eyes and Justice would laugh. "Ok, you can be Batman and I'll be Robin. We're a dynamic duo all the same." Liberty would then lick Justice's nose and Justice would giggle. They were quite a pair – one you wouldn't want to mess with if you were on the wrong side of the law.

It was summer so there was no school. Justice and Liberty had slept in. Finally, Mom woke them up with the alluring scent of bacon. If was a temptation neither could resist.

"I say we go downstairs and start our day the right way," Justice told Liberty.

Liberty was already at the bedroom door, tail wagging, waiting for his boy to let him out.

"Can't go down without this," Justice announced as he put a red, white, and blue cape on his furry best friend. "You know today is the Fourth of July!"

Justice tied the cape securely, opened the door, and they both dashed down to the breakfast table.

"I thought I might see two bright, shiny faces if I fried up some bacon," Mom greeted. "Dad went in to work for a few hours. When he comes home, we thought we'd all go watch the parade. There are street games afterwards and plenty of hot dogs and snow cones. Then, tonight, there'll be fireworks."

Justice was so excited; he could hardly stand it. His

small hometown parade was always so much fun. All the businesses sponsored floats. They always tossed out candy as they drove past. The street games were a blast too. Justice hoped he'd see some of his friends from school. He also hoped he would NOT see and that was Tommy Trip, the school bully. Although Justice and Liberty had put a stop to his shenanigans, they knew he might go back to his old ways and any moment.

"I think Mayor Jones is going to ask you to help with the fireworks, since you have an iron fist and all," Mom informed, shoveling bacon onto Justice's plate. She turned to Liberty. "Sit," she commanded. He obeyed and got a nice, thick slice of bacon too.

Justice smiled. "Sure, I'm happy to help," he replied. His iron fist made it difficult to do some tasks, like handwriting essays at school and tying his shoestrings. But for other things, like launching bottle rockets and shooting fireworks off, it was handy. Should the fireworks get out of hand (literally), he could always rely on his freezing powers.

Mayor Jones had always been very good about publicly crediting Justice and Liberty when they scored against crime. In fact, his son, Hayden was one of Justice's best friends. Hayden was a small kid though he was eleven like Justice.

Tommy used to pick on Hayden until Justice and Liberty put an abrupt stop to it. Since then, Mayor Jones had a soft spot in his heart for the "Dynamo Duo" as he called Justice and Liberty.

Mom cleared her throat and pointed to Justice's plate.

"Better eat some of those scrambled eggs along with the bacon. You never know when you'll be needing your protein…I hear it fuels superpowers."

She laughed but Justice knew she was serious. She took her job as superhero nutritionist to heart and tried to make sure both her boy and his dog were properly fed each and every day whether they had a mission going or not. And as far as Justice knew, they did not have one…not yet, at least.

After lunch, Dad came home from work. Justice knew he was tired, but he tried not to show it. Dad loved spending time with him and his mom. Although he wasn't Justice's biological father, he was his Dad in all respects of the word. He loved Justice as his own and vice versa.

"Ready to roll?" Dad asked.

"Sure!" Justice answered, adjusting the red, white, and blue cap Dad had gotten him.

Dad pulled out a sack. "Oh yeah, forgot to give you this."

Justice smiled and began to open the sack. Inside was a box and inside the box, a pair of top-of-the-line star spangled tennis shoes.

"Thank you, Dad," Justice said, trying on the shoes with a grin plastered on his face. He loved getting new shoes. Even though his dad bought him new tennis shoes all the time, he was always excited to get them and never forgot to let Dad know how much he appreciated them.

Justice stuck out his foot that was clad with blue shoes with red and white stars on them. "These rock!" he determined.

"They're limited edition, so take good care of them," Dad informed. "We'd better get going. Oh...but first, a little something for Liberty." He reached in his pocket and pulled out a treat in the shape of a star. Liberty gobbled it down and the family was on their way to Town Park.

CHAPTER TWO

Bark at the Park

Justice and his parents reached the park just in time for the parade. Dad got the lawn chairs out of the truck and set them up just past the side walk where the parade passed. Mom brought cold drinks and snacks. Liberty stuck his paw out and a treat was delivered to her. "Good girl," Justice told her as she sat beside his chair.

The town parade was always a treat. The town businesses went to great lengths to make it awesome each year. The music began, compliments of the high school marching band. One of the band members was Justice's neighbor friend, Paul. He waved and Paul waved back, not missing a beat on his drums. Paul was a few years older than Justice but always included him when the kids on the block got together for a game of flag football or a friendly baseball game.

"Wow...you should go pro!" Paul once told him. "It's like you have an iron fist when you pitch."

Justice laughed. "I do have an iron fist," he said. Paul wasn't sure if Justice was kidding or not. Justice was not.

Justice noticed the top of the band member's hats had holes in them. "I think it's time for the school to spring for new uniforms," Mom giggled.

Once the band passed, the Ladie's Auxiliary float was next. The eight ladies rode in a pink convertible Cadillac. The wore pink outfits and pink gloves. As they got right in front of Justice and his family, their back tire went flat.

Dad ran out and stopped the traffic while he changed the tire for the ladies.

"That's odd," one of the women told him. "These are brand new tires."

"Must've run over a nail or something," Dad dismissed. But when he got back to his seat, Justice could tell he was concerned.

The ladies tossed out candies. Justice and the other kids ran to gather pieces of gun, Tootsie rolls, Jolly Ranchers, and peppermints.

The next attraction was a club of community members who owned vintage vehicles. Justice always loved checking out the old cars and trucks. It was one of his favorite things about the parade and he also liked that they always tossed chocolate candy bars to the kids.

As he was scooping up a handful of chocolate bars, Justice saw some of his friends from school. "Hey, Charlie!" he greeted.

"Hey, Jus," Charlie returned.

"Wanna come watch the parade with me and my family?" he asked. Charlie had been a family friend since he was a young boy.

"Is Liberty with you?" Charlie asked.

Justice smiled. "Of course," he answered, pointing to his dog who was sitting by his chair.

"Then, yeah…how could I turn down a chance to see my favorite superhero dog?"

Charlie went over to tell his parents he was going to sit with Justice and his parents then came over to join them. Dad got a spare lawn chair out of the car.

"Did you hear about the school break in?" Charlie asked as he petted Liberty. "Oh, that's a dumb thing to ask the crime fighting kid."

Justice was puzzled. "No, I didn't hear about it," he told his friend. "I wonder why no one told me. What happened?"

"You didn't see the band hats?" Charlie asked. "Remember, my brother is in the band…and Paul. So, I got some inside info. The police are just now finding out. No one knew about it until the band met at the school this morning to get ready for the parade. Their top of their hats was cut and some of the music equipment was vandalized. Didn't you notice the tubas were off key?"

"I did notice," Justice said. "I thought they were just out of practice."

Charlie shook his head. "No, man. They had dish soap all in them. I guess that was to make them blow bubbles but all it did was make them sound bad."

"Really bad," Justice added.

About that time, the first float was going past. It was the vetmobile. Every year, the local vet clinic showed off some of their favorite clients. Liberty was always invited to join in but since Justice never knew if they'd be needed for an emergency, he politely declined.

This year, Justice noted how all the dogs and cats riding in the vetmobile were very colorful. There was a pink Poodle, a purple Chiwawa, and a rainbow-colored Lab. Liberty gave Justice a disapproving glance. Justice had the feeling that something was going on...something very sinister.

The vet and staff tossed out doggie treats. Justice let Liberty go get his own. He could always trust her to get a treat or two and come right back.

By the time the next float began to pass by, Liberty still wasn't back. "Where's Lib?" Charlie asked.

Justice looked up and down the street where the parade was routed. He didn't see Liberty anywhere. "I don't know," he answered. "She doesn't just go wondering off. Either someone got her...or..."

"Mon, Dad, we've got to go find Liberty," Justice said as he grabbed Charlie's arm and whisked him down past the oncoming floats. He was beginning to get frantic. Liberty could be in grave danger. He'd just die if something happened to his best friend.

As the firetruck passed, Justice thought he smelled smoke. "Do you...?"

"Smell smoke?" Charlie finished the sentence for him.

"Yeah...," Justice replied. "Something's fishy."

"Smokey, you mean?" Charlie asked.

"That too…but don't you smell that stench? Smells like… fish," Justice said, holding his nose. The he took a good look at the fish market float that was right behind the firetruck float. As it neared, Justice noticed that there were dead fish on top of the float.

Mr. Jackson, the owner of the fish market, waved and tossed some candy to the boys. Justice pointed to the top of the float. Mr. Jackson leaned over the railing and looked. His eyes grew wide and his smile disappeared. Justice felt horrible for him.

Then Mr. Jackson pointed to the firetruck in front of him. It was on fire!

Justice ran over to it, leaving Charlie behind. He saw the fire was coming from the engine. He called for the driver to stop. Once he had, Justice pulled the hood open with his iron fist and put a freeze on the fire.

The driver and the rest of the firemen jumped out of the truck and finished putting out the fire with a hose. "Thank you, Justice," the driver cried. "You are truly our town hero."

"Do you think there is something fishy going on?" one of the firemen asked.

Justice pointed to the fish on Mr. Jackson's float. "I'm pretty sure there is," he answered. "And Liberty is missing. I've got to go find her."

The firemen started the truck and pulled it over to the side. Mr. Jackson pulled his float to the side and began to retrieve the dead fish. Charlie caught up with Justice. They had to find Liberty.

In the crowd, Justice notice Tommy…Tommy the Bully.

"Are you thinking what I'm thinking?" Charlie asked.

Justice took a good long look at Tommy and then began to walk through the crowd over to where he was standing. "I don't like to draw conclusions," Justice answered. "But he's got a shady past, so I've got to check it out. Liberty is lost and I can't take any chances."

No sooner had Justice said that than he heard a bark. It wasn't just any bark…it was Liberty's bark. He pushed through the crowd until he got to where Tommy was. Right beside him, on a leash was Liberty.

"There you are, dude," Tommy said. "Liberty looked lost so I held him here for you."

Justice didn't trust Tommy at first but after a few minutes, he realized Tommy really did have Liberty's best interest at heart. He unleashed Liberty and gave him a hug.

"I was so worried, Lib," he sighed. Just as he did, Liberty took off.

CHAPTER THREE

Things Get Saucy

Justice was right behind Liberty and Charlie was right behind Justice. The faster Liberty dashed through the crowd, the faster Justice and Charlie chased behind him. Finally, Liberty stopped at Bad Barry's BBQ stand.

"Bad Barry?" Justice asked Charlie. "Every heard of it?"

"Nope," Charlie answered. "Smells good though."

A chubby man with a straggled gray beard came to the counter and stared at Justice. Liberty began to bark and bark...and bark. The man's mouth flew open as if he had just realized who the duo was. He ducked behind the counter. Justice knew something wasn't right so he crawled up on the counter to see what the man was doing. But...the man was gone.

Justice heard a door slam in the back. Liberty ran around the BBQ stand and then flew to the grassy area behind it. Justice and Charlie trailed but the man jumped in a truck and sped away. Liberty attempted to chase the truck but it disappeared leaving nothing but dust.

Liberty let out a howl. "You did all you could little boy," Justice assured, patting his precious pup. "At least now we know who's wreaking havoc all over town...I guess. It's Bad Barry."

"Somebuddy call me?" a man asked. Justice turned around to see an Asian man with a blue apron on. "Pardon?" Justice asked.

"Bad Barry...the BBQ guy...that's me," he introduced, sticking out a hand with red sauce all over it. "Oh, 'scuse the mess...tastes good though."

"If you're Bad Barry, who was the man with the gray beard in your BBQ stand?" Justice asked, scratching his head.

"Huh?" Barry questioned. "I just ran to the outhouse for a minute. No body was..." He took a second look at his stand. "Why's the door wide open?"

Barry ran to his stand. The boys and Liberty followed.

"Nooooo!" Barry wailed when he went inside. "Look...BBQ sauce is all over everything. And my money...it's gone!"

Barry let Justice inside the BBQ stand. Everything was in disarray with BBQ sauce all over the floor and counters and the cash register wide open...and empty. A mom, dad, and two children walked up to order some food. Barry hesitated and then told Justice, "I guess I'd better clean up and try to make more money."

Justice agreed. He helped Barry wipe up the mess. Once the family had been served, Justice told his new friend, "I will get the bad guy no matter what I have to do."

Justice felt horrible that he couldn't stop the bad man. He

could tell Liberty felt bad about it too. Since he couldn't drive and the man had sped away in his get-away truck, his hands were tied…in a way. He regretted not at least trying to freeze the man. Everything had happened so quickly though. Now, he was left to figure out clues so he could keep trying to bring the man to justice.

He was sure it was the same person who had vandalized the school band, put dead fish on the fish market float, flattened the tire of the pink Cadillac, and caught the firetruck on fire. But…why?

"Don't you think you'd better check in with your parents?" Charlie asked. "I'm sure they're worried. And if my parents find out I'm not with your parents, they'll be worried too."

Justice knew Charlie was right. He called Liberty and the three walked back to the parade area. Everyone was picking up their lawn chairs and there were no more floats going down the street. Justice found his parents and explained what had happened.

"The parade had to be called off early," Mom informed Justice. "There were too many floats that had been ruined or tampered with. But the street games will go on and the fireworks are still set to go off when the sun goes down, Mayor Jones announced."

"Is it alright if we do some investigating during the street games?" Justice asked his parents.

"Sure," they said. "Just be careful."

Justice agreed to be careful. He, Charlie, and Liberty walked around, looking at the street games and checking out the people.

Every year on the Fourth of July, the main street where the parade took place was closed off so kids could play fun games. There were water balloon tosses, three-legged races, sack races, and so much more. At three o'clock sharp, the firemen always opened the fire hydrant and kids got to play in the water. Charlie wondered how the events of the day were going to go with the vicious activities that had taken place, vandalizing the floats.

Just as the three walked by the water balloon toss booth, they noticed one of their friends, Hayden Jones, getting a water balloon to toss. When he threw it, it splattered onto the street. Instead of water, it was filled with red liquid that looked like blood. Hayden screamed and everyone came running.

Justice hated the sight of blood. He hated his friend being scared even worse though so he walked over and checked out the red liquid. "It's not blood," he assured. "But someone went to a lot of trouble to make it look like it was. It's actually…BBQ sauce!"

Had Justice not known better, he would have automatically thought the prank was the work of Tommy the Bully. But Tommy had obviously learned his lesson the past summer when he had picked on Hayden. Justice and Liberty had intervened.

Justice looked up and saw Tommy talking to Hayden. He eased closer to make sure everything was alright. "I know that must have freaked you out," Tommy was saying. "It would have freaked me out too. Justice and Liberty will find out who is doing all these bad things though. While they are investigating, you can hang out with me. I'll keep you safe."

Justice's heart was warmed by Tommy's offer. He was twice Hayden's size and was quite a bit bigger than Justice too. Although he didn't have superpowers like Justice did, he was a good person to have on your side. Hayden agreed to hang out with Tommy so Justice, Charlie, and Liberty walked on, gathering clues along the way.

CHAPTER FOUR

Where There's Smoke, There's Fire!

Justice was sad the Fourth of July celebrations were being botched. Everyone was still trying to have a good time, but he knew they were proceeding with caution. It seemed like they were all waiting for the next bad prank. No one could enjoy the festivities when they were afraid of what might happen.

As he, Charlie, and Liberty were canvassing the grounds, Justice noticed a crowd was gathering around the firetruck. "Let's go check it out," he told Charlie.

The two boys and Liberty went over to the firetruck, but the firemen were shewing everyone out of the way. "The truck may explode at any time," he warned.

"I'm practically fireproof," Justice reminded them. "Charlie, you'd better stay here. Liberty, you can come with me… you're pretty much a bionic dog."

The firemen let Justice approach. "We are checking to make sure there's not a bomb in here," they informed. "We don't trust anything anymore. The problem earlier was that there was a smoke bomb under the hood. It could have caused the entire truck to blow. That's a felony offense. Hope we find whoever did it, Justice. We are counting on you."

Justice was honored the whole fire department was counting on him. At the same time though, it made him nervous. He wasn't used to having to track down the villain. The fact that the bad man left in a truck made it even more difficult.

After looking over the few clues left behind in the fire truck, Justice went back and got Charlie. They walked around the grounds with Liberty, pretending to mind their own business, but they were really IN everyone's business. They were scoping out every single person they came across. Maybe the bad man didn't act alone.

The street games were still going on. Tommy and Hayden were doing the three-legged race together. "I'm so proud of Tommy for turning over a new leaf," Justice told Charlie.

Even though Tommy was big and tall and Hayden was short and small, they worked beautifully together and won first place. Justice went over to congratulate them.

"We owe it all to you," Tommy admitted. "If not for you, I'd still be a big bully."

"But, you're not and that's what matters," Justice told him.

"What are you three up to?" Hayden questioned. "Haven't seen you playing any of the street games."

Justice paused then explained, "We are looking for the criminal who has been vandalizing all the floats, the fire truck, and even the BBQ stand."

"Oh…wow!" Hayden sighed. "That's terrible."

"We saw him run off from the BBQ stand – out the back door, taking all the cash and leaving the place a saucy mess. He made off in a truck though."

"What kind of truck?" Tommy asked.

"Hard to say," Justice answered. "it was really old and was a bunch of different faded colors."

Tommy stopped walking. "Did the man have grey hair and a grungy gray beard?"

"Yes," Charlie and Justice replied in unison.

"That's…my dad," Tommy told them.

No one said a word. What could they say? Finally, Tommy broke the silence. "Yeah, he's never been around much. He just got out of prison. He was supposed to come pick me up this morning, but he never showed. Now…I think I know why."

Justice wanted to ask Tommy questions about his father. He wanted to tell him how sorry he was that he had such a low-life dad. But, as he was debating on how to word it all, a truck drove past. It was an old truck that looked like the one the bad guy sped away in except now, it had red, white, and blue streamers on it.

Liberty barked and ran after the truck. Justice called him back. "We have to do this the right way," Justice warned. "We need to catch him in the act because right now, all we have is suspicion and speculation and that doesn't hold up in a court of law."

"Tommy, I'm sorry," Justice finally said sadly. "This isn't your fault, and you are way better than him. You changed your bad behavior. Maybe he will too…one day."

Tommy shook his head. "I dunno. I used to spend a lot of time worrying about it. Now, it just is what it is."

Justice and Charlie both gave Tommy a shoulder hug and went about their business, walking around checking everyone out. They were sure they knew who the culprit was already though. All they had to do was to prove it.

They kept plugging on – down the green grass heading in the direction the truck went. Justice knew if he saw the truck again, he could put a freeze on it. Still, that wouldn't prove the bad man's guilt. "I wonder what his name is," he said to Charlie.

"B.G. is what I think of him as," Charlie replied. "Bad Guy."

Justice wanted to chuckle. He wanted to join in the fun street games. He wanted to enjoy Independence Day like all the other kids were. But, he knew with his super powers came great responsibilities. He wasn't about to let his home town down.

"Hi, Justice," a man's voice called.

Justice turned. It was Mayor Jones. "Him Mr. Mayor," Justice returned.

"And what are you two fine boys up to today?" he asked.

"We are looking for the bad guy who's been causing all the trouble – vandalizing the floats and the fire truck and stealing money from the BBQ stand."

"I knew I could count on you," the mayor replied. "I hope

you catch him. We are worried about the fireworks tonight. My heart can't bear to cancel them…but, I may have to. Safety first!"

Justice nodded. "Yes. Safety first. Maybe we will have him behind bars by then. We do know he's in an old truck with streamers on it."

The mayor turned as white as a ghost. "You mean that truck?" He pointed down the road to a truck with red, white, and blue streamers.

"Yes!" Justice and Charlie said in unison.

Mayor Jones looked confused. "That's Doug. He is new to town and offered to help with all the details of the event today. He's delivering the fireworks right now."

"That's not good," Justice cried as he, Liberty and Charlie took off running towards the truck. They could see Doug putting boxes inside the wooden shed next to the podium which happened to be where the fireworks were always shot off from.

"I think he's up to no good," Charlie said, breathless as they kept running.

"No kidding," Justice agreed.

As they finally got to the shed, Doug saw them. He jumped in his truck and peeled off, leaving nothing but tire marks behind.

CHAPTER FIVE

Tackling Problems

Justice's heart sank. "If I had just gotten there sooner...if only he hadn't seen us...if only..."

"Stop it," Charlie snapped. "You are beating yourself up for things beyond your control. You'd say the same thing if the tables were turned and it was me."

Justice sighed. "You're right. But the next time I see him, he's going down. I'm putting a freeze on him. No more goofing off. I have to protect this town. Now, let's go see what we can find out about the fireworks."

The three walked to the shed. There was a lock on the door but Justice easily cut it with his iron fist. They carefully stepped inside.

Liberty went straight to a box of fireworks. He began to paw the box and wimper. Then he barked and barked and... barked.

"I am sure these are something they aren't supposed to be," Justice announced as he ripped the box open.

The three couldn't believe their eyes when the box revealed fifty sticks of dynamite. "Oh my gosh…the fireworks show would have been total disaster. These look like bottle rockets. But they certainly aren't."

Justice decided they should go get the firemen. They walked back across the green lawn where children were still playing street games. The sun was getting lower in the sky. Justice knew that soon the mayor would have to make a very important decision. He would have to cancel the fireworks or put the town at risk. Justice was sure he knew which one he would choose.

When they reached where the firetrucks were parked, Justice told them about the dynamite. "Let's go check it out, Pete," one firefighter told another.

"I'll come along in case I need to freeze them," Justice said. "We don't want an explosion."

The firemen decided it would be a good idea for Justice and Liberty to come along. "I think you should hang back," Justice told Charlie. "Look! There's Tommy and Hayden. You could stay with them."

"Ok," Charlie agreed.

Justice, Liberty, and three firemen walked over to the shed where the dynamite was. Out of the corner of his eye, Justice saw the red, white, and blue streamers coming from the old truck. He was hoping he'd get closer but once again, it sped away.

Once in the shed, the firemen disassembled the dynamite. They ended up not needing Justice's help. But they were relived to have him there…just in case.

When Justice and Liberty got back to Charlie, he was sitting on the green lawn talking to Hayden and Tommy.

"Tommy has a great idea," Charlie announced.

Everyone looked at Tommy. He turned red from embarrassment. Although he had pretended to be big and bad, he was a shy guy deep inside. "It's alright, we are your friends," Justice assured. "You can talk to us about anything."

Tommy thought for a minute and then proceeded to tell them his idea. "I was thinking that maybe we could get the mayor to make an announcement that I had been hurt and if there were any parents here, they needed to give permission for medical treatment."

At first, Justice thought it sounded too easy. Plus, he wasn't sure Tommy's dad would even claim him. "Isn't your mother here?" Charlie asked.

"Yes. But we could clue her in and have her go home. I'm sure my dad is spying on her anyway," Tommy said.

"Ok, it's sounding more legit as we go along," Justice admitted. "What if we got an ambulance to come."

"Perfect!" cried Tommy.

"How about I go tell my dad so Doug doesn't see you talking to him," Hayden offered.

The plan was all in place. Each kid went to do his part and they met back up as arranged.

"Ok, now you are going to pretend to be hurt as we are playing football in the street," Justice reminded Tommy. "I got a little BBQ sauce from Bad Billy." He slipped Tommy a small container of red sauce.

Hayden rounded up a football and the boys headed out to the street. "Liberty, I know you don't fully understand but...'work'...the is 'work'." Liberty licked Justice's nose. Justice knew he would still be worried about Tommy but hoped he wouldn't take it too hard since he had told him it was work.

Out in the street, Charlie tossed the ball to Hayden. Hayden ran and then threw it to Justice. Justice threw it to Tommy, and they all went in for the pretend tackle. They piled on top of Tommy and as planned; Tommy let out a ferocious scream.

Quickly, Tommy spread BBQ sauce all over his face and some on his jeans.

"Help!" Charlie hollered. "Someone's been hurt...bad!"

A crowd gathered around. Justice felt bad, as if he was lying. But it was work and he had to play the role. He continued calling out for help until finally, an ambulance arrived.

The paramedics had been filled in by Mayor Jones but they played along perfectly. They loaded Tommy up and then called into the crowd, "We need parental permission in order to treat him."

"His mother left," Hayden called. "I think his father is here though. He was helping my dad with the event details."

The ambulance drove up to the podium where Mayor Jones was standing. The mayor turned the microphone on and announced, "We have an injured boy on the site. He needs parental permission to be treated. Paging Doug, my helper man, to the podium. Your son needs immediate medical attention."

As feared, no one came. Justice felt horrible for Tommy. It was like he had been stood up by his father all over again.

But then...a man walked up. His hair was gray and his beard, straggled. "What happened to my son?" he asked, frantic.

Justice couldn't help but see that Tommy looked shocked that his father actually came to help.

"Just sign this paper," Mayor Jones said, handing Doug a medical parent permission slip.

Doug scribbled on it and then looked over at Tommy. "Hey, kid. I'm sorry things didn't work out. Go get yourself taken care of and...I'll give ya a call."

Tommy looked sad all over again. He hung his head down and didn't reply.

Justice wasn't sure what to do. Once again, he had the opportunity to stop Doug with his freeze ability. Or, he could hit him with his iron fist. He had other superpowers up his sleeve too. But until they could prove he was guilty, it was all for nothing.

And then...Liberty looked at Justice and pointed his nose at the bed of the truck.

"Are you sure?" Justice whispered. Liberty licked his nose.

Justice knew he was taking a long shot. If Liberty was wrong, the whole thing would be botched. He had to trust his dog though. And so...he did.

CHAPTER SIX

Dynamite in Sight

Justice positioned himself just right so that he could watch every move Paul was making. He knew he only had one chance to catch the criminal. He kept a careful eye on Liberty, hoping he didn't jump the gun.

The bearded man walked briskly to the truck. Justice expected him to jump in it and make a quick run for it again. Instead, he headed to the back of his truck and stared into the bed of it.

Liberty was getting nervous. Justice could sense it. He wondered what the man had in the truck but most of all, he wondered why. Why was he set on vandalizing the parade? Why did he stand his son up? Taking him to the parade would have been a nice way to get reacquainted. He felt so badly for his friend, Tommy, not having a dad around. He felt even worse that he was about to capture him…or at least he hoped so at least.

Justice's thoughts went back to last year when Tommy was a bully. He terrorized the entire school, especially Hayden who was small and not inclined to stand up for himself or engage in any type of conflict. Justice had witnessed too many times of seeing Hayden get bullied. He and Liberty had put a stop to it. They had to. But he really didn't know if Tommy had truly changed his evil ways or not. Now that he was certain that he had, he wanted the best for him. Deep inside, he knew that bringing his father to justice for his crimes was the right thing to do. It was the only way Paul would stand accountable for his actions. I was also the only assurance that the town would be safe. He drew a long, deep breath and concentrated on his superpowers.

He felt his heart racing, beating strong. His iron fist grew even mightier. His legs seemed like they could run a marathon. Every inch of his being was growing stronger, faster, more superior. He could even see better. He could see that inside the back of the truck were more sticks of dynamite. He had to act quick.

"Go!" he called. Liberty dashed with all he had and reached the back of the truck in no time flat. He grabbed the leg of Paul's jeans and began to tug, furiously growling with every pull.

"Get that dog off me!" Paul cried at the top of his lungs. He was reaching for the truck bed handle but Liberty grabbed his hand.

While Liberty detained Paul, Justice ran over to them. He zeroed in on his freezing abilities. "Freeze!" he shouted.

Just as the words came out of his mouth and the powers were being directed, Paul pulled something from his pocket and threw it. There was a loud boom. Paul screamed, "Look! He's on fire!"

Justice turned to look without thinking. He was afraid one

of the firemen behind him was on fire. The freezing power went right to him. "Oh...no!" he wailed, realizing he had frozen the fireman.

Beside the fireman was a harmless, but loud, snap and pop that Paul had thrown to detour him. Now Paul was running to jump in the truck and the fireman was frozen. "Don't worry, I'll be back to unfreeze you," Justice assured the fireman as he darted to the driver's side door of the truck.

Just as Paul was making yet another get away, Liberty snagged his shoe. He growled and tugged while Justice gained ground. With no time to spare, Justice concentrated as quickly as he could and froze Paul in his tracks – hands on the wheel, ready to take off. Finally, Paul was frozen like ice, unable to move, unable to get away.

With Paul completely frozen, the police arrived. There were five of them. One big burly officer gave Justice a high five. "I knew we could count on you," he said. "Now, let's see what this character has been up to."

The mayor was soon there as well. "I trusted this new comer to help me today and all he did was cause mayhem," he declared, wiping sweat from his brow. "Worse of all, he stood up his son. I have no tolerance for hurting children."

An ambulance drove up. Tommy got out. The crowd gasped. "Don't worry, he's alright. He was helping us catch this criminal," Mayor Jones explained.

The police began to go through the truck. First, they went to the back and unloaded the boxes of dynamite. Everyone was in disbelief.

"How could anyone do this to our little town?" someone in the crowd was saying. "And on the Fourth of July? This holiday is one of the most honored."

After several boxes of dynamite were unloaded, the fire department disassembled each and every one so they could not fire off. Then the police opened the truck doors and began searching.

"Look! Lots of BBQ!" one exclaimed, handing a sack of chicken wings to another officer. "Anybody hungry?"

The crowd chuckled nervously as the officers continued their search.

"Looks like we have dish soap…must be what he used in the tubas and here are scissors, no doubt for cutting the band members' hats up. What a jerk!"

Further digging revealed smoke bombs like the ones in the fire truck and a knife that they assumed was for slashing the pink Cadillac's tires.

"Oh…my!" said one of the officers, holding his nose as he held up a dead fish. "This is absolutely crazy!"

Justice couldn't help but notice that Tommy looked really sad. There was his father, frozen, and all the evidence was being revealed. There was no way around it though. Justice had to be done, no matter the cost.

When the truck was emptied of all the evidence, the police slapped handcuffs on Paul and Justice unfroze him.

"What…what is going on?" he yelled.

"You are being arrested for criminal mischief and a slew of other, more serious charges," an officer informed. "You have the right to remain silent. Anything you say can and will be used against you in a court of law."

"A court of law?" Paul winced.

"I have a question," Justice spoke up.

The officers cleared the way to let him through. As he approached, his heart was beating wildly. "I want to know why you didn't go pick your son, my friend Tommy, up and just bring him to the festivities. You two could have had a nice day together."

Paul looked confused. "Huh?"

Justice was not going to let him get off that easily. "You spent the entire day vandalizing this community event. You could have spent it enjoying your son. You've hurt him enough over the years, being in prison and missing out on his life. You could have made up for some of it by spending time together. Why did you choose to terrorize everyone and everything instead?"

Paul looked down at the ground as if he was ashamed. "I'm mad. I've always been mad. Doing mean things makes me feel better...well, kind of, in a way. No one ever liked me when I was a kid. They bullied me and now, I spend all my time getting back at them."

"You grew up here?" Justice asked.

"No...but it's all the same," Paul replied. "I'm just mean to everyone. You never know. One of the bullies might be here today. And just in case they are, their day was ruined... by me. That's a lot of power, ya know. As for the kid, I'm sorry. I'm a bad dad and that's all there is to it."

Justice turned to Tommy. Tommy stepped up, to Justice's surprise.

"I wish you would change your ways," Tommy told him. "I did. You see, I was mad too. I was mad because you weren't around. I used to cause trouble and bully people... like Hayden here. But Justice and Liberty showed me that I couldn't get by with it anymore. I learned my lesson and now, I have a good life. Well, except for you. You made me really sad today when you didn't show up and now...now I have to watch you be arrested. I just hope you will learn your lesson too."

With that, Paul was taken into custody.

CHAPTER SEVEN

A Fabulous Fireworks Finale

With Doug safely behind bars, Justice, Charlie, Hayden, Tommy, and Liberty sat on the grassy lawn and reflected on the day's events.

"I feel like it's all my fault," Tommy admitted.

The boys were shocked. "Why? You aren't responsible for your father's actions."

Tommy sighed. A tear came to his eye. "I don't know. Sometimes, you just feel ways that don't make sense. I always felt like I was trash because my dad was trash. Now I feel like it's my fault the Fourth of July was spoiled for everyone. It doesn't have to make sense…it's just a feeling."

"Just know that we don't blame you and neither does anyone else," Justice assured. "And we never could have caught him without your help."

Tommy smiled. "Oh yeah, I guess I did do something good."

It was getting dark. Justice wished they were about to watch fireworks. He was always fascinated by the bright sparkling colors in the sky and the loud booms.

Suddenly, the mayor came over the loud speaker. "It's been a long day. Thanks to our local superhero and some of his friends and his dog, our town is safe once again. And, thanks to Justice's parents, we now have fireworks safely brought in directly from the fireworks stand."

The crowd went crazy, clapping and cheering. Fireworks began to shoot off. Justice and Liberty waved and took a bow then held hands with Charlie, Hayden, and Tommy. They were a true team underneath the sky that was lit up in the brightest of red, white, and blue they had ever seen.

"I think we make a great team," Justice told the guys when the crowd quietened down. "I think our next mission should be to try to rehabilitate Doug. Tommy needs a father and it sounds like Doug needs a son. Nothing is impossible when we all work together. Tommy turned from bad to good and I believe his father can do the same. What do you say, team?"

The guys cheered. Liberty barked, and barked, and barked some more. Then she licked Justice's nose and he knew it was just a matter of time that his dream would become a reality.

CHAPTER EIGHT

Independence Day

Justice knew there was one more thing that needed to take place before the Fourth of July could come to a complete close. "Do you want to go see your dad in jail?" he asked Tommy.

Tommy looked surprised. "Hum…I never thought of that."

"I'll take you there," Justice told him. "I just happen to be able to teleport…under certain situations. And, I am pretty sure this qualifies."

Liberty winced.

"Yes, you can go too," Justice responded, giving Liberty a much-deserved treat.

"Well…ok, yeah. I'll go!" Tommy decided.

Charlie and Hayden smiled. "It won't be easy, but it will be good for both of you," Hayden said.

Justice got up and Tommy and Liberty stood beside him. He concentrated with all his might and soon, the three were at the police headquarters.

"We would like to visit Paul," Justice told the officer who was minding the front desk.

The officer led them down a long, dark hallway to a row of empty jail cells. Justice cringed thinking of the criminals who had occupied the cells in the past – some who he himself had helped put behind bars.

In the one at the end of the row was the dirty gray-haired man with the straggled beard who had caused so much trouble all day.

"Hi,…Dad," Tommy began.

"Uhhhh…Tommy?" Paul replied.

"Yeah…I just wanted to say that no matter how bad of a person you are on the outside, I still believe in you on the inside." Tommy's voice was breaking as he finished. "If and when you are ready to change your ways, we can hang out. I would like to get to know you…not the bad you that covers up your feelings and tries to get revenge…. but the real you. I believe there is a good guy in there under all that meanness."

"You do?" Paul asked. He scratched his gray beard and listened.

Tommy shook his head. "Yeah, I do. You see, Justice believed the same thing about me and look at us now. Maybe one day, it will be me and you helping stop crime. We could tell other bad people that we believe in them and help them turn their lives around. You never know what good we could bring to the world. But most of all, I just hope you learn that bad guys always get brought to justice with Justice and Liberty around. With any luck though, they turn out like I di and like you hopefully will turn out too."

Paul wiped a tear from his eye. "I'd like that, son. Let's talk more about it after…well after whatever it is they do to me. I'll give you a call….for real this time. And…"

Tommy listened in as his father continued. "And this time…I'll show up…for real."

Tommy smiled. "I'd love that…Dad," he told him.

Tommy, Justice, and Liberty left the jail. No one said a word for their were no words that could express what had just taken place. Through Justice and Liberty's brave actions, justice had been served. Tommy and his father had finally come to peace. It had been a crazy Independence Day but they all had the feeling it was the beginning of something very good to come.